KIDS CAN'T STOP READING
THE CHOOSE YOUR
OWN ADVENTURE® STORIES!

"I like Choose Your Own Adventure books because they're full of surprises. I can't wait to read more."

—Cary Romanos, age 12

"Makes you think thoroughly before making decisions."

—Hassan Stevenson, age 11

"I read five different stories in one night and that's a record for me. The different endings are fun."

—Timmy Sullivan, age 9

"It's great fun! I like the idea of making my own decisions."

—Anthony Ziccardi, age 11

And teachers like this series, too:

"We have read and reread, worn thin, loved, loaned, bought for others, and donated to school libraries our Choose Your Own Adventure books."

**CHOOSE YOUR OWN ADVENTURE®—
AND MAKE READING MORE FUN!**

Bantam Books in the Choose Your Own Adventure® Series
Ask your bookseller for the books you have missed

Choose Your Own Adventure Books for younger readers

THE MYSTERY OF ECHO LODGE

BY LOUISE MUNRO FOLEY

ILLUSTRATED BY DON HEDIN

An Edward Packard Book

BANTAM BOOKS

TORONTO · NEW YORK · LONDON · SYDNEY · AUCKLAND

RL 4, IL age 10 and up

THE MYSTERY OF ECHO LODGE
A Bantam Book / March 1985

CHOOSE YOUR OWN ADVENTURE ® *is a registered trademark of
Bantam Books, Inc. Registered in U.S. Patent and Trademark Office and elsewhere.*

Original conception of Edward Packard

ISBN 0-553-24720-4

Published simultaneously in the United States and Canada

---

*Bantam Books are published by Bantam Books, Inc. Its trade-
mark, consisting of the words "Bantam Books" and the por-
trayal of a rooster, is Registered in U.S. Patent and Trademark
Office and in other countries. Marca Registrada. Bantam
Books, Inc., 666 Fifth Avenue, New York, New York 10103.*

PRINTED IN THE UNITED STATES OF AMERICA

O   0 9 8 7 6 5 4 3 2 1

For Bill Foley, my Sierra skier
who's special

WARNING!!!

Do not read this book straight through from beginning to end! These pages contain many adventures you can have as you try to solve the mystery of Echo Lodge. From time to time, as you read along, you will be asked to make decisions and choices. Your choices may lead to success or disaster!

Your adventures are the result of your choices. *You* are responsible because *you* choose! After you make your choice, follow the instructions to see what happens to you next.

Strange things have happened at Echo Lodge. You must discover who—or what—is behind them. Think carefully before you make a move. One mistake could be your last.

Good luck!

A light snow is falling the December morning you arrive at the Lake Tahoe bus station. As you leave the bus you stare at the majestic peaks of the Sierra Nevada range. This is going to be the best winter vacation you've ever had. Aunt Sadie said there'd be lots of time off from your duties at her lodge to go snowmobiling and to learn how to ski.

You enter the depot and look around. Aunt Sadie's bellman, Russell Lyons, is supposed to pick you up. A small man is seated on a bench, reading a newspaper. He's wearing a heavy plaid jacket and a cap with ear flaps, and his navy trousers have gold stripes down the legs.

"Excuse me," you say. "Are you Russell from Echo Lodge?"

Slowly the newspaper is lowered. The man stares back at you through wire-framed glasses. He looks about eighty years old.

"So Sadie found me another city kid to train," Russell says. "Cheap help. That's what happens when you go broke. Not like the old days. Come on!"

You follow Russell outside and climb into an aging purple van with SADIE'S ECHO LODGE printed in gold on the side.

"Who's going broke?" you ask as he shifts it into gear.

"Sadie's going broke," Russell says. "More cancellations than reservations these days. I know it's the Paiute jinx!"

He suddenly steers off the main highway onto a narrow mountain road.

Turn to page 3.

What's the Paiute jinx? you wonder. You hesitate to ask Russell. He seems so crabby. Maybe Aunt Sadie will explain. You ride in silence, staring at the rugged mountains and deep canyons.

"Here it is," Russell says, pulling up in front of a steep stone flight of stairs. The main lodge, almost hidden by towering pine trees, is a two-story structure of stone and redwood. A stone chimney climbs one wall, and around the main building are four small chalets. Their steep, sloping roofs support a heavy snow pack, and dagger-sharp icicles hang from the eaves.

"Go on up," Russell tells you. "I'll park the van."

You drag your bag up the steep stairway and enter the lobby.

"Aunt Sadie?" you call, peering around. Your aunt comes running in.

"Just call me Sadie," she says, giving you a hug. "You got here just in time. My switchboard operator quit this morning."

As Sadie hustles you into her private suite of rooms you notice a small blond woman in a red dress staring at you.

"Furthermore," Sadie whispers, slamming the door, "last night we had a power failure, and Countess Maria's diamond watch was stolen. Heidi and I are in desperate need of help."

"Who's Heidi?" you ask Sadie.

"I am," growls a voice behind you. "Who are *you?*"

Turn to page 9.

4

You shuffle off the road, up the slope toward the cabin. If Heidi is in there, she'll be killed by the avalanche.

Through a small cluster of trees you can see a ramshackle building. Propped up against one wall, half covered with snow, is a weather-worn toboggan. You peer in a window; the cabin is dark and cluttered inside. Then you go around to the opening where the door should be.

"Heidi!" you call.

A muffled sound comes from a corner of the room. Heidi is hunched there, bound and gagged. Quickly you take the cloth from her mouth and untie the ropes.

"Am I glad to see you!" she sputters. "That phony medicine man left me here to freeze to death."

"Hawkins is no phony," you say, surprising yourself. "He's a gray shaman and he's dangerous! He's gone to the summit to start an avalanche that will wipe out this cabin and Echo Lodge. He has supernatural powers, Heidi!"

"Tommyrot," says Heidi. "He has that vicious killer hawk. That's how he forced me in here."

"He has that hawk with him?" you ask, surprised by this news. "That means that Russell's in for trouble. He's gone to the summit to find him."

"Let's go," says Heidi grimly.

Turn to page 99.

You run to the left, calling, "Russell! Russell!"

The only answer is your own voice, eerily echoing back. You stand still until the sound fades. There is silence; then your voice is replaced by the moaning you heard coming from the fire.

Very little moonlight seeps through the tall pines, and you can barely see where you're going. You move cautiously ahead, too frightened to return to the site of the fire.

You slip on an ice-crusted patch of ground and grab a branch to regain your balance.

"Over here," a voice whispers. "I've twisted my knee."

You squint through the darkness. Russell is lying in a small ravine that leads down to the stream. You hurry to him.

"You will have to take care of the spirits," he tells you. "And then go to the lodge for help. Now, fill the canteen and douse the fire thoroughly! It is your only hope!"

"I don't think I should leave you," you say, taking the canteen with shaking hands.

"You must!" Russell says gruffly. "Go now. I'll be all right!"

Your hand grips the canteen tightly as the moaning noise from the crag drifts toward you again. As you stumble down toward the stream, it gets louder. Do you have the courage to go back to the crag alone? Maybe you should go directly to the lodge to get help.

If you go back to the crag, turn to page 27.

If you go directly to the lodge, turn to page 94.

You repeat to Heidi exactly what you heard on the phone.

Heidi frowns. "I'll spend the night in the van," she says. "Russell's been using it all day. They couldn't have touched it yet."

After dinner you join Heidi in the van to help her keep watch. It's a long, cold night. No one comes near.

The next morning you eat breakfast in shifts, making sure that one person is always in the van. At ten o'clock you and Russell and Heidi leave for the airport.

"I'll stay with the van while you and Russell are in the terminal meeting the team," you tell Heidi. Secretly you're hoping for a chance to be the hero in this mystery.

Heidi and Russell disappear into the terminal, and you settle down to watch the travelers coming and going. You're sure that one woman, who has just wheeled into the row opposite you, is going to miss her flight. She rams on the brakes, jumps out of the car, and opens the trunk. Grabbing a brown suitcase, she slams the trunk and runs to the terminal. As she hurries off you think she looks vaguely familiar.

You watch a plane coming in and forget about her. Within minutes Heidi and Russell and the ski team return to the van and begin loading luggage. As Russell pulls away you notice the woman backing her car out. She must have missed her flight.

Turn to page 60.

You whirl around to confront the blond lady from the lobby. Only she's now dressed in a purple flowered muu-muu and is wearing a black wig. You have no idea how she got into the room.

"This is my niece's child," Sadie explains. "Here to help us out through the winter vacation."

"Hmm," says Heidi skeptically. "Can you follow orders?"

"That depends on who gives them," you reply.

"When you work with me, I give them," Heidi snaps. "I am the Echo Lodge house detective. Retired from a long and distinguished career with Interpol—the International Criminal Police Commission."

Her speech is interrupted by a wailing siren.

"Fire!" Heidi shouts. "Fire in the lodge! You evacuate the second floor. I'll get the dining room."

Heidi pushes you toward the lobby, and you race up the main stairs. You bang on doors, shouting, but most of the rooms seem to be empty. When you reach Room 223, you hear a radio playing loudly and the sound of water running.

You bang on the door. No one answers. You try the knob. The door is locked. Should you go to the desk for a key or force the door open? The siren is still screeching.

*If you go to the desk for a key,
turn to page 12.*

If you force the door, turn to page 17.

"I don't believe in shamans or jinxes," you say to Russell. "I'll get Heidi to help me find that hawk."

You leave Room 223 quickly and go downstairs. Heidi is standing at the lobby door, watching a man who looks as if he were waiting for a ride.

"Heidi!" you say. You begin to tell her about 223, but she cuts you off.

"No time for that now," Heidi says curtly. "I think a lot of people are going to be hurt if those two have their way."

She points to a brown truck that has pulled over to the side of the road. The man gets in and the truck drives off. Heidi grabs her jacket from the lounge chair.

"Where are you going?" you ask.

"To Echo Summit. Hurry up!" she says, motioning for you to follow her.

She leads you out to the parking lot, and you both climb into the van.

"Who are they?" you ask as she pulls out of the lot.

"I don't know who the passenger is, but the driver is Flame Mulligan, a munitions expert. In 1963, while I was with Interpol, he wiped out a chalet in Switzerland."

"Why?"

"Money," she replies, steering around a sharp curve. "He was hired by a rival chalet owner."

"Did he blow it up?" you ask.

Turn to page 71.

"I don't believe in vanishing birds or haunted rooms," you tell Russell. "I'm going back up."

You turn and head for the main stairs. Russell follows you, but a woman in a fur coat grabs his arm as he moves across the lobby.

"You can put the luggage in my car now," she says.

Russell's frightened eyes meet yours, but he can't stop you. When you get to the top of the staircase, you look back and see him struggling out through the door with the woman's suitcases.

You hurry down the hall and stop in front of 223. You don't recall shutting the door, but it's closed now. You try the knob. Locked. You'll have to go to the desk for a key.

You're turning to go back downstairs when you hear a soft rustle on the other side of the door. Your heart starts to pound. Someone or something is in there. Try again, says a voice in your head.

You put your hand on the brass knob. This time it turns easily. Slowly you push the door open.

You don't believe what you see. Russell is seated at the desk. You freeze in the doorway.

"How did you get here?" you ask haltingly. "I just saw you going outside with that lady's luggage."

"Come in," Russell says, staring at you. "Close the door and sit down. I will tell you about the gray bird."

If you close the door and sit down, turn to page 62.

If you run back to the lobby, turn to page 100.

You run downstairs to the empty lobby and scan the row of mailboxes behind the desk. There it is! 223. With luck there'll be a spare key in the box. Your hand closes around something metallic. But what you hold is not a key. It's a woman's diamond-studded wristwatch. It must be the one stolen from the countess! Hastily you shove the watch in your pocket and whirl around to face the switchboard.

You think you can figure out how to work it. If you ring 223, maybe the occupant will answer. You slip on the headset and start to plug a cord into the 223 outlet. But there's already a cord plugged in! You open the switch.

"We'll have Sadie out of business by spring," a man says. "Tomorrow, when Russell brings the ski team from the airport, you will arrange for them to have an accident. They'll be riding in the van." He laughs. "It will be the van's final run."

The next thing you hear is a dial tone. Just as you yank off the headset, the siren stops. The guests file back inside. You must tell someone what you overheard and about finding the watch. But who? Sadie is already nervous about things going wrong. You could tell Heidi, but you're not convinced she's competent. She seems a little strange.

If you choose to tell Heidi, turn to page 15.

If you choose to tell Sadie, turn to page 25.

"I want to stay and work with Heidi," you tell
Sadie. "I don't believe in death threats or jinxes."

Sadie sighs. "Please be careful," she says.

"Let's go, kid," says Heidi. "We have work to
do."

You follow her out through the back door to the
parking lot.

"First thing for you to do is wash the van," Heidi
says.

"That doesn't sound like detective work to me,"
you mutter.

"We all have to start somewhere," Heidi snaps,
handing you a bucket and a sponge. "Get busy."

You have worked only a few minutes when you
hear a strange cry coming from the forested area
across the road. You can't see anyone, but you
hear it again. It sounds as if someone were hurt.

You throw the sponge into the bucket and run
across the road, crashing through the low shrub-
bery. Deeper and deeper into the forest you go,
led on by the cries. Finally you stop.

When you stop, the cries stop too.

Turn to page 23.

Heidi has just entered the lobby and is talking to one of the guests. She's dressed in a cowgirl outfit, complete with lariat.

"Heidi!" you whisper, grabbing her arm. "I just heard—"

"Go to the laundry room and count the bath towels," Heidi tells you. "Here's the key."

"But . . . but . . ."

"Go!" says Heidi, pointing down the hall.

You unlock the door marked LAUNDRY and enter. Angrily you start counting. You're up to sixty-eight when the door opens.

Heidi enters and closes the door behind her. "Good work," she says. "You can follow orders. Sorry about sending you off like that, but I had to get you out of the lobby. Did you notice the man I was talking to? Mr. Yarman?"

You shrug. "Sort of," you say.

"You'll have to work on being more observant," she says, frowning. "I think Yarman is causing Sadie's problems. I didn't want him to hear whatever you had to say. It sounded urgent."

"It is urgent," you say. "I just overhead a phone conversation saying that the ski team is going to have an accident on the way to the lodge tomorrow. Maybe someone's going to tamper with the van. Oh, and I found this too. It was in 223's mailbox." You hand her the wristwatch.

"I know about the watch," Heidi says. "I put it there. Found it in Yarman's room this morning. But the news about the ski team worries me. What exactly did the caller say?"

Turn to page 7.

You put your hand on the doorknob, brace your body, and slam into the panel. As you make contact the door to 223 flies open, and you sprawl on the floor. Someone unlocked the door! And they did it while you were standing there!

But there's no one in the room. You get up from the floor. The radio is still blaring, and you can hear water running in the shower. Quickly you kick the room door shut. You remember that fire rule from school safety classes.

"Fire!" you yell, banging on the bathroom door. "Everyone out!"

There is no reply, so you push the door open. The shower stall's glass door is ajar. Water is flooding out. A feather floats on top of the water. You turn off the tap, pick up the feather, and grab a folded towel from the rack.

As you toss the towel into the water on the floor, something drops from its folds. You crouch down and pick up what looks like a small piece of bone.

That's when you hear it. A soft whirring behind you. Still half crouching, you awkwardly turn toward the sound. Hovering on top of the door is a gray hawk. Its amber eyes are trained on you, as if waiting to attack. Instinctively you throw your arm up to protect your head as the bird rockets toward you. Its sharp talons tear into your arm, and you lose your balance, sitting down hard in the layer of water on the floor. By the time you get back on your feet, the bird has flown to the other room.

Turn to page 28.

You put on the snowshoes and follow Russell. The climb is difficult. Eventually you reach another turnout in the road. Hawkins's car is parked off to the side.

"Maybe Heidi's still in there," you say, hurrying over.

"I doubt it," says Russell. "She'd follow him as far as she could. But she has no snowshoes."

Russell is right. The backseat of the car is empty.

"There's an old cabin up that slope," he says, pointing off to the right. "I think that's where she'll be. I want you to go to the cabin, get Heidi, and go back to the van."

"But what about you?" you ask.

"I'm going on to the summit to deal with Hawkins."

"Not alone!" you protest, staring at the small elderly man. "You can't handle Hawkins alone! You can't stop an avalanche!"

"I will not be alone," Russell says quietly. "My spirit animal will stalk him with me. Go to the cabin now. Hurry! It will be in a direct line with the avalanche aimed at the lodge." Without waiting for you to answer, he shuffles up the road.

He's so old, you think as you watch him disappear around a turn. He can't handle Hawkins alone! Heidi may not even be in the cabin. What should you do?

If you go to the cabin to look for Heidi, turn to page 4.

If you follow Russell to the summit, turn to page 64.

You stand steady, watching Hawkins approach.

"Call off the hawk!" you yell at him. "I want to talk."

Hawkins nods. "The spirit hawk has yet another task to do," he says, raising his arms toward the leaden sky.

Surprised and relieved, you watch the hawk immediately fly out over the canyon, higher and higher, until it disappears.

"I want to talk," you repeat.

Hawkins glides closer. "It is too late for words," he says. "The white bird is already preparing for flight." His black eyes flash wildly. "The power of nature cannot be stopped."

He's crazy, you think. How can you reason with a madman? If only Russell would come! What could have happened to him?

"Russell is also a shaman," you say boldly. "He is here. Now. On the mountain. He will counteract your evil."

Go on to the next page.

A sneer crosses Hawkins's face. "The spirit hawk has been sent to stop Russell's meddling," he says. He reaches to his belt and pulls out a curved knife. Your hopes for rescue by Russell fade.

"Move," says Hawkins. "Down there." He points to a ledge below and to the left of where you're standing. "The white bird will meet you there."

The clumsy snowshoes make running impossible. You half slide, half walk, down the steep incline. Below you on the slope is a dilapidated building. That must be the cabin Russell talked about. Beyond that is the cluster of buildings that make up Echo Lodge.

Hawkins *is* crazy. He's sending you directly into the path of the avalanche!

Turn to page 114.

All you hear is a faint rustling to your right. Frightened, you swing around. A gray hawk is watching you from the branch of a pine. Your heart pounds. You push on into the forest. The cries start up again. Only when you stop do they stop. And each time you stop, the hawk appears—silently waiting and watching.

Night comes to the forest. You're getting tired. But you dare not stop, knowing the hawk will come. The cries are driving you crazy. There's no peace!

By the time you're found, you have lost your mind.

The End

The next day you and Heidi talk to the police.

"We won't have any trouble picking Yarman up," the officer says. "He has no reason to hide. He thinks Heidi's dead, and he arranged her death to look accidental. That's why he sent one of her skis down the mountain."

"Why did you go with Yarman?" you ask Heidi. "And who is he?"

"Yarman had a gun on me. That's why he made me drive," she explains. "He's a banker from San Francisco. And part owner of the Maple Leaf Inn, Sadie's biggest competitor. He was trying to ruin her business. He overheard you tell Sadie you found the countess's watch in my mailbox, and knew I was on to him. You see, I found the watch in Yarman's room this morning."

"Well, I guess I'm out of a job," you say.

"No, you can still work the switchboard. And next year, I want you working security with me. I think you're a natural."

"Will you teach me how to ski too?" you ask.

"Sure," says Heidi, patting your cast. She grins. "I *know* you're a natural at that!"

The End

"Sadie!" you say, hurrying over to her. "I found the countess's watch in Room 223's mailbox!"

"That's odd. Two twenty-three is Heidi's room," says Sadie, taking it from you.

A quick thought runs through your mind. Maybe Heidi stole the watch. Maybe she's causing these strange things to happen.

"That's not all," you say to Sadie. "A man on the phone said the ski team is going to have an accident tomorrow on the way from the airport to the lodge."

"An accident?" Sadie whispers. "It's the Paiute jinx again."

"What jinx?"

"Last year, when I was making plans to build the North Chalet, I got a note in the mail saying that the site of the building was sacred tribal ground. It said the lodge would be haunted by evil spirits if the chalet was built."

"You don't believe it, do you?" you ask.

"I didn't then, but I don't know now. Russell belongs to the Pit River tribe. He thinks we can't ignore it."

"Well, I think someone's going to tamper with the van," you say. "Do you want me to guard it?"

"No," Sadie says. "I'll have Heidi do that. I want you to make up the rooms or help the chef. Which do you want to do?"

Neither job sounds like fun, but you don't want to upset Sadie any more than she already is.

If you make up the rooms, turn to page 38.

If you help the chef, turn to page 74.

You steel yourself to return to the crag. You crack the ice at the stream's bank and dip the canteen in the frigid water. Then you climb back out of the ravine and head for the crag. The moaning gets louder. The fire is eerie. Blue flames lick at the rocks, and at the center, a fountain of orange sparks leaps into the air.

Quickly you throw the canteen's contents at the sparks. The instant the water hits, the flames die. The moaning stops. All that is left is a frozen pile of gray ash.

On the way back to Russell you pick up a sturdy branch.

"I'm not leaving you here," you tell him. "We can make it if you lean on me and use this for a cane."

Your descent is slow. As you approach the lodge parking lot you see a group of guests standing by the North Chalet.

"What's happened?" you ask.

"The strangest thing," Sadie says. "We heard this terrible moaning noise, and when we came out to investigate, a hawk was flinging itself at the chalet window." She points to a bird lying dead on the snow and shudders. "It beat itself to death."

She looks closely at you and Russell. "Where have you two been? And why is Russell using a cane?"

"It's a long story," you say. "Russell can tell you when we get inside and get his knee bandaged."

The End

Wrapping a clean towel around your arm, you hurry back into the room after the hawk.

But the bird is nowhere in sight! You check the closet and under the bed. The hawk has disappeared. It can't be! The door is still closed—and locked. The windows are not only closed, but are covered on the outside with storm windows.

Suddenly the siren stops. The lodge is quiet.

And in the silence you realize that another oddity has occurred. The radio that was blaring when you entered the room is also quiet.

You leave the room and hurry downstairs. Your arm still hurts. In the lobby Sadie is talking to a muscular, dark-haired man who looks angry. Russell is standing beside some luggage at the main entrance.

You approach Sadie. "I have to talk to you, Sadie," you say softly.

"Not now!" she replies. "I'm talking to Mr. Hawkins."

"Sadie! This is important!" you whisper.

She brushes your hand from her arm.

You feel so helpless. Something strange is going on. You've got to find out who was booked in 223 and who owns that dangerous bird. It must be caught before someone else is attacked. Should you interrupt Sadie again? You glance toward the door. Russell might be able to help.

If you approach Sadie again, turn to page 72.

If you ask Russell, turn to page 47.

"Yes," you say to Russell. "I'll go to Lovers' Leap with you tonight."

"Good. Meet me by the storage shed. And don't say a word to anyone!"

That evening, when the clock in the lobby chimes seven, you grab your jacket and go to meet Russell. He is carrying a lantern and a coil of rope, and a backpack is strapped to his shoulders. He hands you a pair of snowshoes.

You wind the leather thongs over your boots and awkwardly take a step.

Russell smiles. "You will get used to them," he says as he starts up the trail at the back of the lodge.

Turn to page 52.

"What's a shaman?" you ask Russell.

"A medicine man with supernatural powers," he tells you. "We of the tribe call Hawkins a gray shaman. He uses his power for evil. He's threatened to use the spirits against Sadie."

"Why?"

"He claims she built the North Chalet on sacred ground. At one time this was all tribal land."

"You don't really believe in the supernatural and spirits and shamans and all that, do you?" you ask him.

"I do," he replies. "And so should you. The hawk that attacked you—that was Hawkins's spirit bird. It is through the hawk that he gets his power." He pauses. "Hawkins claims immortality."

"But that's unreal!" you protest.

"That which is unreal is also real," Russell says.

"Well, why does Sadie let him stay at Echo Lodge?" you demand.

"Fear," he replies. "Last year, when she refused him a room, the roof on the East Chalet collapsed."

"Well, I don't believe in gray shamans or pink shamans or—"

"Neither does Heidi. That's why she's in danger. Interpol tactics cannot stop a gray shaman."

"Then what can?" you ask sarcastically.

"Only another shaman," Russell replies, seriously.

Go on to the next page.

You stare at him, and slowly the realization sinks in.

"I am a shaman of the Pit River tribe," Russell says, nodding. His gray eyes lock with yours. "I'm going after Hawkins, but I'll need help to rescue Heidi. Will you come?"

If you agree to go with him, turn to page 101.

If you decide not to go, turn to page 68.

Later, at the police station, you learn that the man you tackled is really co-owner of the Maple Leaf Inn, Sadie's biggest competitor. He and Flame Mulligan make a complete confession about sabotaging Sadie's business.

"So there was no Paiute jinx," you say to Sadie when you get back to the lodge. "Your problems were definitely caused by humans, and not by spirits."

Sadie looks at you solemnly and holds out her arm. As she pulls her sweater sleeve back, your breath catches in your throat.

Sadie's arm bears the talon marks of the hawk.

The End

34

You're in a parking lot, next to an old car. "Get in the backseat," orders the man with the gun, climbing in after you. Karen and the other man get in front.

"Where are you taking me?" you ask, trying to sound calmer than you feel.

"Tell the kid, Al," says Karen to the driver.

"Everyone who comes to Tahoe should visit the lake," Al says with a sneer. "We're going to take you for a little boat ride."

"It's December!" you say. "The lake will be frozen!"

"Tahoe never freezes," he says. "It's too deep 'n' ornery."

He steers the car down a side street to a docking area.

"Out," says your seatmate, poking you with the gun.

Turn to page 40.

"Leave the cat alone!" you say to the chef. "He's sick!"

"Out, out!" the chef yells, grabbing the box and setting it outside.

His actions infuriate you. "He was fine until he ate your soup!" you snap. The minute you say it, the pieces fit together. Karen put something in the soup. Something dangerous. And disappeared.

"How dare you say that!" the chef yells angrily.

"Wait a minute," you say, grabbing his arm. "I think Karen put something dangerous in the soup. I think that's why the cat got sick. He was drugged."

"Nonsense," says the chef. "Get back to work."

"No! You've got to warn the guests. They can't eat the soup!"

"I'll do no such thing!" he says. "It's my reputation!"

"Well, I will," you say.

"If you do, Sadie will find herself without a chef to prepare the evening meal," he threatens.

You don't want to make things worse for Sadie. Maybe it wasn't the soup that made the cat ill. But maybe it was.

If you warn the guests, turn to page 37.

*If you start scrubbing potatoes,
turn to page 105.*

You march away from the chef and into the dining room.

"Hold it, everybody!" you shout. But you're too late. The diners are slumped in their chairs, unconscious.

"What's happening?" Mary asks you.

"Karen drugged the soup," you reply.

"Why?" she asks.

"I think our answer is coming in the door right now."

She turns to follow your gaze. Two masked men are holding the chef at gunpoint. They motion for you and Mary to come.

"Sit down," says one of the men in a muffled voice.

The three of you sit at an empty table.

"Watch them while I get their lunch," he says to the other man.

In a few minutes he comes back from the kitchen with a tray. On it are three bowls of soup.

"Eat," he orders.

Turn to page 41.

"I guess I'll make up the rooms first," you tell Sadie.

"Fine," she says, handing you a ring of keys. "The linens are in the laundry room, down the hall by the switchboard."

You hurry to the laundry room. You're fumbling for the right key when you hear a soft click. Someone is inside! You press yourself flat against the wall in the shadows as the door opens.

Heidi steps out of the laundry room and walks past you. Why was she in there? Puzzled, you enter the laundry room and pull some towels from the shelf. When you do, you uncover a telephone jacked into a wall panel. Could Heidi have been the other person on 223's phone? You did find the watch in her mailbox! Maybe she's secretly working against Sadie.

You go back to the lobby. Heidi is standing by the fireplace, talking with a blond man who looks like a weight lifter. They're both dressed in ski clothes. Is that man her accomplice? you wonder. As you watch them Sadie comes out of her suite.

Go on to the next page.

"Sadie!" Heidi says. "Mr. Yarman wants a ski lesson. I'm going to take him to Redwood Ski Ranch for the afternoon."

They're not going to ski, you think. They're going to make more plans to sabotage Echo Lodge. It may be rude to invite yourself, but you're not going to let them get away.

"Can I go too?" you ask Sadie. "I want to learn how to ski."

"Oh, I guess so," she says. "We don't have any new guests coming in today. There are some ski clothes in my suite."

The man glowers at you, and Heidi looks very uncomfortable.

Turn to page 51.

"Too bad you can't see Lake Tahoe in daylight," Karen taunts. "It's lovely. But who knows? Maybe you'll survive till morning."

Al pushes you toward a large launch at the dock. You board and the others follow. Within minutes the motor is growling. The craft trembles as it heads out on the dark lake.

"Why are doing this?" you ask, pulling your collar up around your ears. "What have you got against Sadie?"

"Nothing personal," says the man with the gun. "It's strictly business. The winter trade at Tahoe won't support both Maple Leaf Inn and Echo Lodge, so Echo Lodge has got to go."

The air is bitingly cold. You know Tahoe is the second deepest lake in the country. And cold. If they're going to throw you overboard, you might be smart to jump now, before you get too far from shore. You're a good swimmer. You might make it.

If you choose to jump, turn to page 90.

If you stay in the launch, turn to page 110.

When you regain consciousness, Sadie is standing over you. The lodge is in chaos. Some guests are still groggy from the drug; some are recovered and furious; all have been robbed. Heidi is on the phone to the local police.

By nightfall most of the guests have checked out. Sadie is sitting by the fireplace, checking the guest register.

"The Bryants and the Tompkinses will leave in the morning," she says. "That's everyone but the countess."

"The countess!" Heidi yells. "She wasn't in the dining room!"

"Of course not," says Sadie. "The countess eats breakfast at eleven. She never eats lunch."

Turn to page 48.

The bird is spooky. Its yellow eyes stare at you, unblinking. Very slowly you rise from your crouching position. As you do the hawk moves closer.

You breathe deeply to fight the panic that's racing through your body, and try to inch your way around to the forest side of the circle of rocks. The bird blocks your path. You move the other way. The hawk stops you.

Those yellow eyes are almost hypnotic. You try to break their spell by glancing down at the ground. The minute you do, you wish you hadn't.

In the center of the fire ring you're building is a pile of rattlesnake rattles! Not two or three, but dozens! Beside them lies a large gray feather.

With a shriek you jump up to run. The hawk takes flight, its wings beating furiously around your shoulders and head.

You fling your arm up to protect your face as the hawk's talons reach for your eyes. Screaming, it drives you back toward the edge of the cliff.

Like the Indian couple a century ago, you fall to your death from the crag known as Lovers' Leap. The coroner calls it a climbing accident. Only Russell suspects what really happened.

The Paiute jinx has claimed a victim.

The End

"Yes," Russell says. "The hawk is Mr. Hawkins's source of power."

"Do you think he's responsible for Sadie's problems?"

"I'm sure of it," Russell replies. "He says that Sadie built the North Chalet on sacred ground."

"Did she?" you ask.

Russell shrugs. "I do not know for certain. But I plan to stop his destruction."

"That's Heidi's job," you say. "She's a trained agent."

Russell stares off into space. "Agents are trained for tracking this world's human evil," he says. "The menace that visits the lodge comes from another source and sphere. Heidi does not believe me when I tell her so."

You stare at the small wiry man as he speaks. He obviously believes absolutely in what he is saying. Is he crazy?

Turn to page 50.

Back at the lodge, you're treated for exposure and put to bed.

The next morning you curl up with a blanket in a chair by the lobby fireplace. Heidi confirms that all the guests were drugged and robbed. No one regained consciousness for hours.

When you were finally discovered to be missing, the police put out a bulletin. Fortunately the story was carried on television news, and an alert teenager reported that he saw someone fitting your description down at the waterfront with three adults. After that it was easy. The police were waiting at Al's car when the trio docked the launch.

"I thought for sure I'd freeze to death on the dock," you tell the people who have gathered around you in the lobby. "In fact, I still don't think I'm ever going to get warm."

"I know just the thing you need," the chef says. "A nice hot bowl of soup. My soup is irresistible."

"More than irresistible," you say, grinning at him. "Your soup's a knockout."

The End

"Don't let him get away!" Mary yells.

You dash to the door, chasing the thief, but there's no need for heroics. In his haste, he fails to see the cat in the box on the top step. He trips over it and falls down the short flight of stairs, hitting his head on the last step.

By the time you get to him, he is just as unconscious as the guests in the dining room. You march back inside and call the police.

"The two gunmen made a full confession," the police tell you later. "They were hired by a San Francisco businessman who has money invested in the Maple Leaf Inn—Sadie's major competitor. He was trying to put her out of business."

"My reputation would have been ruined," Sadie says.

"What about Karen?" the chef asks.

"A chemist from the Bay Area," Heidi replies. "The San Francisco police are looking for her."

"Good," he says. "She almost ruined *my* reputation."

"I'm hungry," you say. "Anything good to eat around here?"

"I have a fresh pot of soup cooking," offers the chef.

"Pass," you reply. "I think I'll settle for a candy bar."

The End

"Who was checked into 223?" you ask Russell.

"The haunted room?" he says with a fleeting grin. "Heidi's the only one brave enough to stay in there."

"What do you mean, haunted?" you ask.

"A reporter from San Francisco stayed in there last winter. He heard strange noises. His typewriter was stolen. Went back to the city and wrote an awful article about Echo Lodge."

"Well, he can add an attacking hawk and a minor flood to the list," you say. You show Russell the deep scratches on your arm and explain what happened. As you talk, Russell's expression changes from one of amusement to concern. "And what's this?" you continue, showing him the tiny bone.

Turn to page 57.

"Maybe the countess saw the men drive in!" Heidi says. "The North Chalet overlooks the parking lot. Let's go talk to her!"

You walk the short distance to the chalet. Heidi knocks.

"Come in!" yells the countess.

You push open the door. The countess is watching a mystery on television. Curled up beside her is the black-and-white cat.

"Heidi! That's the cat!" you say.

"Quiet!" says the countess, pointing to the screen. "They're accusing the wrong person! That tall man is the murderer!" She snaps off the set in disgust. "These TV detective stories are so simplistic. A child could solve them. Please sit down."

You and Heidi sit on a low sofa. The cat jumps down and comes straight to you. He purrs as he rubs against your leg.

"My cat likes you," the countess says. "He was lost today for a while. I asked two very unpleasant men in the parking lot if they had seen him, and they almost ran me down with their car."

"The men!" Heidi says. "Can you describe them, or the car?"

Turn to page 54.

"You came to help Sadie," Russell continues. "You will learn my ways, and together we will overcome the evil force."

"Wait a minute!" you say. "I can help Sadie just as much by working with Heidi! I'm not sure I believe all this."

Russell's gray eyes dart to yours. "You have no choice," he whispers. "The hawk has attacked you. You are now its prey. You must work with me, or through you the hawk will destroy Sadie."

Dare you defy him? you wonder. Something is ruining Sadie's business. Is it of this world or another? Has the hawk really targeted you?

If you choose to work with Russell, turn to page 55.

If you choose to work with Heidi, turn to page 10.

It takes you only a few minutes to change into ski clothes.

"You can rent the equipment," Sadie says, handing you money.

You thank her and follow Heidi and Mr. Yarman outside. "We'll take my car," he says to Heidi. "You drive."

You ride in silence to the ski ranch. Heidi and Mr. Yarman wait outside the ski shop while you get outfitted. The sky clouds over as you start for the lifts. There are few skiers on the slopes.

"Here's your lift ticket," says Heidi, handing you a green card. "Pin it on your jacket."

"Getting off a lift is tricky, kid," Mr. Yarman warns. "You be ready when I tell you."

You get into one chair, and Heidi and Mr. Yarman get into the one behind you. The view from the lift is scary. The buildings below look like little dots as you travel up the mountain.

Suddenly Mr. Yarman yells, "Ready! Jump off now!"

You seem to be too far from the ground, but you do as you're told. You pitch forward into the snow. Mr. Yarman tricked you! The lift is continuing up the mountain, and he and Heidi are still on it!

You're not hurt, but the force of your fall unfastened the pin on your ticket. You start to pin it back on your jacket when you see something red on the back. HELP—written in lipstick!

Then Heidi's not a conspirator . . . and she needs help!

Turn to page 76.

52

"Tell me the story of Lovers' Leap," you say to Russell as you begin to climb the trail.

He nods. "A century ago a Paiute warrior and a Washo maiden fell in love. The Washo and the Paiute had been enemies for centuries, and the couple was forbidden to see each other. So they found a secret meeting place at the top of this crag. One day they were observed by a Paiute scout. That night they entered into a pact. Rather than be separated in life, they chose to be together in death. With arms around each other they leaped from the top and fell to their death hundreds of feet below. Their bodies were found on the site where the North Chalet now stands."

You shudder and scramble up the last few feet in silence.

"I'll gather some kindling," Russell says. "You build a circle of rocks to enclose our fire."

He disappears into the forest, and you work by the light of the moon, arranging loose rocks into a circle. Suddenly you become aware of something near you. You turn slowly. A large gray hawk is sitting motionless behind you.

Your first impulse is to run after Russell, but your logical mind tells you that the hawk's appearance is just a coincidence.

If you try to get rid of the bird, turn to page 93.

*If you stay on the crag with the bird,
turn to page 43.*

"Of course," says the countess. "I was trained from a child to be observant. The car was a green two-door sedan with a dented right front fender, two rearview mirrors on the sides, and leopard upholstery. Nevada license number XVID530."

Heidi grins. "Countess, tomorrow you're going to get breakfast in bed. Compliments of the house!"

"But not before eleven, darling. And please send some kippers for Sherlock," she says, stroking the cat lovingly.

"Sherlock," you mutter. "That figures."

The End

"I'm not sure I understand all this," you tell Russell. "But I want to help Sadie. What do you want me to do?"

He stretches his gnarled hand toward you. Lying in his palm is the piece of bone you found in Room 223. "You must destroy this," he says.

"So it's not just a piece of plastic," you say, taking it from him.

"No," he replies. "It's a rattlesnake rattle. The Paiutes used them in burial rites. They carry death if they're not destroyed after the ceremony."

"Death?" you say.

"Death," Russell repeats somberly. "Death to the one who finds it. We must have a cremation ceremony tonight. We will go to Lovers' Leap. We must burn the rattle on sacred ground."

"What's Lovers' Leap?" you ask, frowning.

Russell gets up and goes to the window. "Up there," he says, indicating a sheer-faced crag that looms above the road. "I'll tell you the story tonight."

"How do we get there?" you ask, not eager to hear the reply.

"We climb," he says. "But not the face. There is a trail on the north side that has served my people for centuries. Meet me behind the lodge at seven."

You shiver. Dusk is already casting black shadows on the mountain peaks, and the wind is howling. The rational part of you rejects his explanation.

If you agree to go, turn to page 29.

If you refuse to go, turn to page 75.

Russell quickly reaches over and takes it from your hand. "Who knows?" he says. "A broken piece of plastic from something." He forces a grin. "Maybe you hit your head when you fell on the wet floor. Instead of seeing stars, you're seeing birds!"

"Then explain this," you say angrily, holding out the feather.

His eyes dart from the feather to your face.

"Just a feather," he says, reaching for it.

You pull your hand back before he can take it. "I know it's a feather," you say disgustedly. "Obviously you're not going to tell me what's going on. I'm going back up to 223. Somebody has to look for that bird!"

"Don't go!" Russell says. "It's the jinx. Let Heidi go up."

What's he afraid of? you wonder. Is the room really haunted?

If you go back to 223, turn to page 11.

If you go to find Heidi, turn to page 80.

You row feverishly toward the lights. There's a dock at the water's edge, a rope ladder hanging over its side. You climb up quickly and run to the building. A man in uniform answers your knocking.

You're at a forest ranger station! The man hustles you inside and gets hot tea and a blanket. While you're warming up you tell the ranger and his partner your story.

They exchange glances, obviously puzzled.

"Don't you believe me?" you ask. "Do you know who the man was who told me to go to the west side? And who's Nancy? I never found her."

"You found her," one ranger says slowly. "The *Nancy* was the boat that brought you here. And the Englishman was Captain Dick—Richard Barter—a hermit who lived on the island for many years. He built the chapel too."

"Well, we'll have to return his boat," you say.

"I'm afraid that's impossible," says the ranger gently. "Captain Dick was drowned one blustery night, when the *Nancy* was driven off course. That was over a hundred years ago. They never found his body—or his boat."

Turn to page 69.

"I just had another phone call," Sadie says, hurrying over to you and Heidi.

"The death threat again?" Heidi asks.

"Yes," answers Sadie. "Only this time *I* wasn't threatened." She looks at you.

"A threat against me?" you ask, your heart pounding.

"Yes," whispers Sadie. "Your life may be in danger. You must leave the lodge at once."

"Wait a minute," says Heidi. "Let's be rational about this. If you let those conspirators convince you that the Paiute jinx is real, you'll be out of business before the end of the season."

"I can't risk it!" Sadie says. "Russell says that shamans have great power. And there was a hawk upstairs!"

"What's a shaman?" you ask.

"A member of an Indian tribe who has supernatural powers," Sadie explains. "Mr. Hawkins is a shaman. He gets his power from his spirit animal—the hawk. That's why I wanted to get him out of the lodge quickly."

"Do you think it was Hawkins who threatened me?" you ask.

"I don't know," Sadie says wearily. "It's your choice. Do you want to stay . . . or go home?"

If you decide to stay, turn to page 14.

If you decide to go home, turn to page 89.

The van is crowded, so you sit on the suitcases for the trip back to the lodge.

"Maybe the phone call was just to scare us," Heidi whispers.

You're puzzled too. You shift position on a suitcase and wonder what could happen now. Suddenly you know.

"Who owns this brown suitcase?" you ask the skiers.

Several shake their heads. One shrugs. No one owns it!

"Stop the van, Russell!" you holler.

Quickly you slide the door open. You grab the suitcase and heave it over the side of the road, down into the canyon. Halfway down it bursts into a ball of flame.

"Whew!" says Heidi. "How did you know?"

You explain about the woman at the airport. "It was Yarman in disguise," you tell Heidi. "I knew her face looked familiar. Yarman must have just added the suitcase to the skiers' pile of luggage."

"He's one of the owners of the Maple Leaf Inn," Heidi says, "Sadie's biggest competitor. They wanted her out of business." She pats your shoulder. "You're pretty observant, after all."

"I'm working on it," you tell her.

The End

Slowly, keeping your eyes on Russell, you close the door to 223.

"Come. Sit down," he repeats.

"I don't get it," you say, inching your way into the room. "What do you know about the hawk? And how did you get up here so quickly? And why were you frightened when I showed you that piece of bone?"

"You may choose not to believe what I am going to tell you," Russell says. "Heidi does not believe. Sadie only sometimes.

"That man you saw downstairs arguing with Sadie—Mr. Hawkins. He is a shaman, a person with supernatural powers. Hawkins is what we of the tribe call a gray shaman."

"Is that like a medicine man?"

"In a way," says Russell. "Only much more powerful. Shamans can heal both the body and the spirit. But gray shamans use their power for evil and destruction."

"You said, 'We of the tribe,'" you say. "Are you Paiute?"

"No," Russell replies. "I am of the Achomawi—the Pit River tribe. My grandfather was a shaman."

"And you?" you ask nervously.

"I, too, have the power," Russell says quietly.

"Where do you get this power?" you ask, not believing, but fascinated by what he's telling you.

"The power comes from nature—a bird, a tree, an animal."

"The hawk," you say. "The hawk must be Mr. Hawkins's power."

Turn to page 44.

Certain that you won't survive by the shore, you leave the dock and head for the forest. Around its edge the wind has blown the snow into low drifts. You're glad you have the flashlight. You pick your way through the underbrush.

It's warmer in the shelter of the pines, and you push on until you come to a bare patch of ground. It looks like a good place to make a bed. You can't walk any farther. You're exhausted. If you cover yourself with branches, you may survive till morning.

You doze off, giving only a fleeting thought to any wild animals that may be around. But your subconscious grabs that thought and turns it into a nightmare. You awaken with a start, sure that you heard something rustling nearby.

You jump up and move on, pushing through the trees until you come to a small clearing. The light from your flashlight flickers on a small wooden building that looks almost like a chapel.

You move closer. It looks very old—maybe a hundred years or more. There is no covering over the windows, and the door is partly open. Weeds growing over the step fill the entry.

The building will certainly be warmer than a bed of pine needles, even if it does look spooky. You squeeze through the doorway and look around. The inside is bare except for a wooden altar on a raised platform at the front.

You sit down in a corner and doze off. But not for long.

"Cheerio, matey!" says a voice from nowhere.

Turn to page 83.

You give Russell another minute's lead and then start up the road after him. When you reach the top ridge, you can see no one. Maybe you should have gone to the cabin! The wind whines as it whips the snow into your face.
You're wondering which way you should go to find Russell when suddenly, from behind, you hear a shrill scream. You turn quickly and look up.
The gray hawk is circling above you, and with each circle, coming closer.

But even more frightening, you see Hawkins approaching you on skis from the far side of the ridge.

You look quickly to the stand of scrub pines to your left. The trees will give you some protection from the diving hawk, but none from Hawkins. Should you try to reason with him? you ask yourself. Maybe you can talk him into calling off the bird.

If you try to reason with Hawkins,
turn to page 19.

If you try to reach the pines, turn to page 79.

You stop and turn around. The voice didn't sound familiar, but you're going to need help from someone.

A security guard, holding a flashlight, approaches you. "Who are you?" he asks. "And what are you up to?"

Quickly you explain what happened. "I think everyone at Echo Lodge was drugged with that soup and then robbed."

"You're right," he says. "The word is all over town. Come on inside, and we'll find out who booked the room that you were held in. Can you identify the woman?"

"I sure can," you say, following him in through a back door. "What is this place anyhow?"

"Maple Leaf Inn, in South Lake Tahoe. I'm a guard here."

He leads you down the hall to the lobby. Behind the registration desk there's a door marked PRIVATE.

"Go into the executive suite and wait," he tells you, pointing to the door. "I'm going to check the guest register."

Go on to the next page.

You open the door and enter. A TV is blaring in the living room, but there's no one around. You go over and curl up in an easy chair to wait.

"You're pretty tricky, kid," says a voice behind you.

You turn around. Karen is standing by the chair, smiling.

"We're going to take a ride," she says as two men come from the kitchen. One of them is holding a gun.

"Get moving," says the man with the gun, pushing you out a rear door off the kitchen.

Turn to page 34.

"No," you say to Russell, "I think Heidi can take care of herself. Nobody made her get into that car. Besides, I don't believe the hawk was a spirit bird. I think it's somebody's pet, trained to attack."

"Then I will go alone to stop the flight of the white bird."

You frown. "It wasn't white," you tell him. "It was gray."

"The bird I seek is white," Russell says. "And will be found near the summit." He turns and leaves the lobby without another word.

At dinner that evening Sadie notices that Russell and Heidi are absent. "I wonder where that pair went," she says. "I like to have them around during these winter storms. One radio station was even predicting an avalanche at the summit."

"Russell's gone to the summit," you tell her, between bites. "To stop the flight of the white bird."

Sadie turns to look at you. "The white bird?" she repeats. "Mr. Hawkins mentioned a white bird when he checked out."

"What did he say?" you ask, beginning to feel concerned.

"I think he said, 'Swiftly the white bird flies at night.'"

Turn to page 88.

"But I came in the *Nancy!*" You jump up and run outside, down to the pier. The rope ladder dangles over the side, its fraying ends dipping in the rhythmic cold waves of Lake Tahoe.

There is no boat.

"Come on. I'll take you to the authorities," says the ranger, putting his arm around you. "If you can identify your kidnappers, you can at least help solve one mystery."

The mystery of your rescue from Emerald Island remains unexplained, but for the rest of your life you believe in ghosts.

The End

"No," says Heidi, "he buried it."

"Buried it?" you repeat, puzzled.

"Avalanche," says Heidi grimly. She points to the brown truck parked at the side of the road and pulls in behind it.

On a ridge above, you can see the two men working over some equipment.

"I'm going to circle around behind them," Heidi says. "Get as close to them as you can and make some snowballs. When you hear me whistle, start throwing."

"If you whistle, they'll know where you are!" you say.

Heidi grins. "Not on Echo Summit."

You creep toward the men and prepare your ammunition. Heidi disappears from sight. When you finally hear her whistle, you know what she meant. The shrill sound comes from all directions, echoing over and over.

You start pelting the men with snowballs. They run in different directions. Heidi tackles Flame Mulligan, but his partner heads for the truck. You lob a snowball off his ear, but he keeps going. You've got to stop him. An idea flashes into your head.

"Get him, Harry!" you yell. "Sam! Grab him from behind!"

Your words echo, coming back from all directions. The man whirls around, trips, and falls in the snow. With a flying leap you land on top of him and hold him down until Heidi brings you a piece of rope.

Turn to page 33.

"Sadie!" you interrupt. "There's a hawk on the second floor!"

"I'll have Russell take a look," Sadie mutters. "Mr. Hawkins is checking out. Take his luggage out to his car."

Angry at being so quickly dismissed, you grab the bag and stride from the lobby out to the parking lot. Hawkins follows.

"Put the suitcase on the backseat," he tells you.

You open the door, and that's when you notice them.

On the floor in the back is a gray feather and beside it, several bonelike objects—just like the one you found in 223.

Mr. Hawkins is watching you with narrowed eyes. You know he saw you looking at the bones and the feather. And you know he didn't like it. You put the bag in and slam the car door. He doesn't offer you a tip.

You go back to the lobby and march over to Russell.

Turn to page 82.

You turn into the forest to the right.

"Russell!" you yell. Your voice echos over and over through the forest and dies away, leaving only a throbbing in your ears.

Suddenly a shadow crosses your path. Someone is walking on the trail toward you. You freeze in terror.

"Dumb city kid. Cheap help!" the person mutters. It's Russell!

"I think I heard Heidi scream," you tell him. "What's she doing up here?"

"Checking on us," Russell mumbles. "I found her on my way back from dousing the fire on the crag. She's got a sprained ankle. She's over here." He turns off the trail and goes through some low brush.

"Do you think the Paiute jinx has been broken?" you ask.

"Don't know," Russell says. "We'll see what happens tomorrow. Get me some branches."

Turn to page 85.

"I'll help the chef," you tell Sadie, and head for the kitchen.

The chef is standing by the stove, stirring soup in a large pot. A young woman stands at the sink, scrubbing potatoes.

"Sadie sent me to help you," you tell the chef.

"Another greenhorn," he grumbles. "Here. Stir this. I have to make a phone call." He hands you a spoon. "And no sampling! You get to eat after the guests, not before."

He must be reading your mind. It smells awfully good, and you're hungry. As the chef goes out through the swinging doors the young woman moves from the sink to the stove.

"I'm Karen," she says, grabbing the spoon from your hand. "I'll do the soup. You get over to the sink and scrub the potatoes."

You frown. Who's in charge here? you wonder.

"Are you hungry?" Karen asks.

As you turn to answer she takes a sip from the spoon and wrinkles her nose. "Not bad," she says, "but it could use some more seasoning." She reaches into her apron pocket and pulls out a salt shaker, muttering, "Let's dress this up a bit.

"Aren't you hungry?" Karen asks again.

"The chef said . . ." you start to say.

"Don't worry about him. What he doesn't know won't hurt him. Do you want some?"

If you say yes, turn to page 95.

If you say no, turn to page 78.

"No," you say to Russell. "I'm not willing to go. It's crazy to climb a mountain at night in a blizzard because of a curse that I don't even believe."

"Have it your way," says Russell. He looks at his watch. "We've talked through the dinner hour. Go down to the kitchen and get something to eat. I have to repair a window in Room 246."

You hurry from the room and go downstairs to the kitchen. As you enter, the smell of chicken greets you, and you realize that you haven't eaten for hours.

"Aren't you Sadie's relative?" a waitress asks.

You nod.

"Sit down here," she says, pulling a stool up to the counter. She sets a steaming plate of chicken and dumplings in front of you, and you dig in. "Russell told me you'd be eating late."

You look up so quickly that the food sticks in your throat.

How did Russell know you'd be eating late? you ask yourself.

Turn to page 87.

Heidi needs help now! You've got to try to ski down.

The wind is blowing flurries of snow, and the sky is gray. You bend your knees and push off. It's scary as you gain momentum. You're doing better than you thought, but you're not prepared for the tree that looms up in your path.

You panic. You don't know how to change direction! You try swerving to the left, but you're not quite quick enough.

The ski patrol finds you two hours later and transports you back to the ski lodge. When you try to convince them that Heidi and Mr. Yarman are still up on the mountain, one of the ski patrolmen reassures you that he saw Yarman an hour ago, at the lodge. A doctor gives you a shot to ease the pain of your broken leg, and you're loaded into an ambulance. As it pulls away you hazily see the face of Mr. Yarman. He is smiling. And he is alone.

Sadie meets you at the hospital. "Why did Heidi leave you?" she asks. "Mr. Yarman called and said that he wouldn't be returning, that he had urgent business in San Francisco. He asked me to send on his luggage. He said he left you and Heidi skiing."

"I think Heidi's still at the top of the mountain," you tell Sadie. "You'd better call the ski patrol. Maybe you can convince them that she's still up there. I couldn't."

Much later that night, in the midst of a raging Sierra blizzard, another patient is admitted to the hospital. It's Heidi—nearly frozen to death.

Turn to page 24.

"Not I," Russell replies softly, "but the power of nature. Hawkins died in the evil he created, in the avalanche."

"What is your spirit animal?" you ask as you snowshoe toward the cabin.

The question is barely out of your mouth when you see the snow ahead of you spattered with blood and littered with gray feathers. Leading away from the spot, heading toward a wooded area, are the paw marks of a mountain lion.

You look into Russell's gray eyes.

"My spirit animal is the mountain cat," he replies softly.

"It killed the hawk!" you say.

"No," Russell tells you. "The spirit can never be killed."

He points to the leaden sky. Directly above you a hawk is circling. Higher and higher it flies, until it vanishes.

The End

"No, thanks," you say to Karen. "I'll wait till the guests have eaten."

When the lunch bell rings, Karen hands you a ladle and points to a stack of empty soup bowls. "Here," she says. "Dish out the soup while I check something."

As she opens the back door a skinny black-and-white cat races into the kitchen and jumps up on the counter.

"No!" you yell at the cat. "Get out of here!"

But it's too late. The cat has smelled the soup and is already lapping some from a bowl. You put down the ladle, pick up the cat, and set him down on the floor.

"Go crawl under a table," you mutter, "and no one will mind."

You're filling the last three bowls when you notice the cat is staggering as if he's dizzy.

Mary, the waitress, comes in from the dining room to get the soup. "Better get that cat out of here before the chef catches him," she says, picking up a tray of bowls.

"Okay," you say. You bend over to pick up the cat. But as you do, he takes a few uncertain steps and collapses on the floor.

You pick up the cat and put your ear to his chest. His heart is still beating. What's wrong with him? you wonder. He's definitely sick. Quickly you find a box and make a bed for the cat. You're sliding it under a counter when the chef comes in.

"What's that cat doing in my kitchen?" he yells.

Turn to page 35.

You shuffle as quickly as you can toward the scrub pines. You're aware that Hawkins's skis will move much faster than your snowshoes. You glance back to see where he is.

Hawkins has stopped! He is no longer following you, but is standing still on the ridge. The hawk, too, has given up its attack. It is sitting on Hawkins's shoulder. As you watch, Hawkins turns and skis off in the other direction.

You heave a sigh of relief. So much for magic and supernatural powers, you think. Now if you can just find Russell and get back to the van. Maybe he's found Heidi and they've already gone back to the rest area where the van is parked. You feel so dumb. How could you ever have believed all that shaman nonsense?

Turn to page 92.

"Where's Heidi?" you ask Russell.

"Probably in the dining room," he says.

You hurry into the dining room. It's deserted. Wondering where to look next, you go to the picture windows that give the diners a spectacular view of the mountains. Below you is the winding road that you came in on. A car is parked at the foot of the steps. Someone is climbing into the backseat. It's Heidi! You watch as she pulls a blanket over herself and huddles on the floor. What's she doing? Whose car is it?

You don't wonder for long. As you stand there Mr. Hawkins storms down the steps, gets behind the wheel, and drives off.

"What are you staring at?"

You whirl around at the sound of Russell's voice.

"Heidi," you say. "She just left in Mr. Hawkins's car."

"Hawkins's car?" he says. "Did he force her to go?"

"No," you tell him. "She hid in the backseat."

His face becomes a mask of fear. "I told her he was dangerous," Russell says. "She didn't believe me."

"Who is Hawkins?" you ask.

"Hawkins is a Paiute shaman," Russell answers. "A gray shaman."

Turn to page 30.

You turn around quickly. Heidi is standing there, dressed in an Indian sari. A jewel hangs in the middle of her forehead.

"There's a hawk up there and a flood in Room 223," you say.

"And I suppose Russell thinks it's the Paiute jinx," Heidi says, smiling.

"I don't know what he thinks," you reply. "What's the Paiute jinx?"

"A little over a year ago," Heidi says, "when business was good, Sadie had plans drawn up for the North Chalet. Soon after, she got a letter, supposedly signed by Mr. Hawkins, saying that the site of the new building was a sacred tribal ground of the Paiutes. That terrible things would happen at the lodge if she started construction."

"She obviously didn't believe it," you say. "At least she went ahead with the building."

"Russell tried to talk her out of it. He's a member of the Pit River tribe, and he believes in shamans and jinxes and things like that. But I convinced her to go ahead with her plans. I think someone is just using the threat of a jinx as a convenient excuse to force Sadie out of business."

"Who would do that?" you ask.

"I suspect it's the owners of the Maple Leaf Inn," Heidi replies. "They're Sadie's biggest competitors."

"Does Sadie believe in the jinx?" you ask.

Heidi's answer is interrupted as Sadie hurries toward you.

Turn to page 59.

"Who is Hawkins?" you ask. "And do you know what this is?" You pull the bonelike object you found in 223 from your pocket.

"It's a rattlesnake rattle," Russell whispers. "It's bad luck. Where did you get it?"

"It was hidden in a towel in room 223," you tell him. "And there's a vicious gray hawk flying around up there too. Look." You show him the deep scratches on your arm.

A look of concern crosses his face. "Stay here," Russell says. He hurries across the lobby and takes the stairs two at a time.

"Haven't seen old Russell move that fast in a long time," says a voice behind you. "What's the crisis now?"

Turn to page 81.

"Cheerio, matey!" the voice repeats.

You struggle to shake yourself awake. It takes a few minutes to realize where you are. You look around the chapel. Of course, there's no one here! You're dreaming. You close your eyes again.

"Take Nancy and go back to the mainland," says the voice in a clipped British accent.

You wave your flashlight into the corners of the chapel. There's nothing. Nobody. But you know you're not dreaming!

"You can make it!" says the voice. "Shake a leg, now! Nancy's waiting on the west side."

You stumble over the doorsill back outside. West, you think. Which way is west? You were abducted on the east shore, and you crossed the lake. That means you came west in the launch.

Just keep going through the forest, you tell yourself. The island can't be that big. Your mind is full of questions. Who is Nancy? Who is the Englishman?

Suddenly you break through the trees. Ahead of you, in its vast darkness, is the lake. You trace the shoreline with your flashlight. You see no one, but the beam catches on a pier to your left. And bobbing in the water by the pier is a small boat!

You run to it. It seems sturdy enough. It's not taking on water. You lower yourself into the little boat and grasp the oars. Directly across the water you can see land. It's the west shore of Lake Tahoe—and a building with lighted windows!

You forget how cold and tired you are and row toward the lights.

Turn to page 58.

Puzzled, you do as you're told, and then watch in amazement as the elderly man expertly lashes them together. He gently helps Heidi onto the makeshift toboggan and starts easing it downhill.

"Where did you learn that?" you say, striding beside him.

"I train the Sierra ski patrols," he says. "You thought I was just a superstitious old man, didn't you?"

You're glad it's dark, so he can't see your embarrassment.

"That's all right." Russell chuckles. "Sometimes cheap help turns out to be okay. Might give you a few ski lessons, too, if you stick around long enough."

"I'd like that," you tell him.

The End

Jumping here would be suicide! You can't fly, but the chickens can. You pivot around so the men in the station wagon can't see what you're doing. Hastily you unwire a cage and lift the mesh screen door.

"Get going, birdies," you say, shooing the chickens out.

Startled, they flap their wings and awkwardly fly toward the traffic that's following the truck. Two of them swoop toward the window of the station wagon, squawking loudly.

You open another cage and release more chickens.

Horns honk. Traffic stops. The truck driver rams on the brakes. Eventually, two highway patrolmen on motorcycles glide in between the stalled cars.

Turn to page 98.

You sputter and choke as the waitress rushes to the sink to get you some water. But water is not going to dissolve the bone that is frozen in your throat. Your air passage is completely blocked. You slide from the stool to the floor.

By the time a doctor arrives, it is too late. Your death is the final blow for Sadie. She boards up the lodge and moves to San Francisco.

"It's strange," the doctor testifies later at the coroner's inquest. "But I never saw a chicken bone that looked like this. If I didn't know better, I'd say it was a rattlesnake rattle."

The End

The disaster is the lead item on the eleven o'clock news that night. The Reno television station reports:

"At 8:23 tonight the popular Echo Lodge resort was wiped out by a killer avalanche that roared down from Echo Summit. The only survivors were the house detective and the chief bellman, who were both away from the lodge at the time the avalanche struck."

The End

"I think I'll go home," you tell Sadie. "I wouldn't believe any of the death threat or jinx stuff if that hawk hadn't attacked me upstairs."

"I'll feel better if you're safe at home," she says.

That afternoon Russell puts you on a bus for home. You stare out the window for a long time, lost in your own thoughts, as the bus lumbers down the winding highway.

The driver's voice brings you back to reality. "Placerville!" he announces. "Fifteen-minute rest stop!"

You follow the other passengers into a coffee shop. You're sitting at the counter, staring absently out into the street, when you see someone across the street who looks familiar. You stand up for a better look.

It's Heidi! And she's being forced into the front seat of a red station wagon by two men. You catch a glimpse of metal as one man slides a gun under his jacket. You rush out, but the car pulls away. But not before you see the decal on the back of the wagon. Inside a white circle is a green maple leaf, and beside it, neatly lettered in gold: MAPLE LEAF INN—SOUTH LAKE TAHOE.

Those are the people Heidi thought were sabotaging Sadie! They must have found out that she suspected them.

Across the street is a rickety truck, just starting to pull out from the curb. The door panel says: SMITH'S CHICKEN FARM, SOUTH LAKE TAHOE.

"Hey!" you yell at the driver. "Can I hitch a ride?"

Turn to page 115.

You grasp the launch's siderail with both hands and take one last look at the shoreline. Some flickering lights are still visible. You muster all your strength, and before Al or the man with the gun can act, you vault over the side.

You hit the frigid water with a crash.

There is no gunshot. No confusion. No attempt to stop you. Only the high-pitched sound of Karen's laugh, ringing out over the water.

The launch turns around and heads for shore. Hypothermia is swift. You sink quietly to the icy depths of the lake that's six thousand feet above sea level and surrounded by the grandeur of the Sierra Nevada range.

The morning sun breaks in glorious color on Tahoe, "Lake of the Deep Water." But you don't see it.

The End

Even as you stand there thinking, you feel a strange sense of foreboding. You look up. The hawk is sitting motionless at the top of one of the pine trees, watching you. Beyond the bird, up the slope, you see a wall of white gliding toward you. Panic-stricken, you try to run. But there is no place to go!

The only sign of life remaining after the avalanche hits is a solitary hawk circling the area where a grove of scrub pines once stood.

The End

You crouch there, staring into the yellow eyes of the hawk. You move slowly to the left. The bird follows. You move right. It follows again. You must outwit this golden-eyed predator.

Your hand closes around one of the rocks in the circle. Suddenly, with a wild shriek, you jump up and lunge to the right, throwing the rock as you do. The bird takes flight instantly, and you wheel around and run into the forest.

Russell has heard you yell and thrashes through the underbrush toward you. Breathlessly you tell him about the hawk.

"Quickly," he commands. "We must build the fire quickly before the hawk comes back."

He thrusts his backpack at you, and you hurriedly dump the pinecones and needles it contains into the rock fire ring.

As Russell strikes a match to the needles you fish in your pocket for the rattle.

"Throw it in!" he says. "Hurry!"

There is a fountain of sparks as you toss in the rattle. A strange, almost human moaning drifts up from the blaze. Frightened, you look over at Russell.

"Water," he whispers, backing into the forest. "I'll go to the stream. We must drown the spirits!"

He disappears, and seconds later you hear a scream, echoing over the canyon. It sounds like a woman's voice. You jump up and run after Russell. Another scream—from deep in the forest. It sounds like Heidi! Suddenly the forest is silent.

Turn to page 104.

You're not going back to the fire site alone. And besides, getting help for Russell is more important. You circle around him so he won't know you're disobeying his orders and start down the slope to the lodge. The wind is stronger now, and snow stings your face. The moon has disappeared, and it's hard to find the trail under the fresh snowfall. When you finally reach the lodge, you're exhausted.

Heidi goes with the ski patrol to rescue Russell, and Sadie sends you to bed with a hot-water bottle.

In the morning you come down to the lobby long after breakfast has been served. You feel a twinge of guilt when you see Russell sitting in an easy chair with his leg on a footstool.

"Are you all right?" you ask him.

He looks at you sadly and nods. "You didn't drown the spirits," he says. "Tonight after sundown you must return alone to Lovers' Leap and finish the job"—his voice drops to a whisper—"if you're still alive."

You open your mouth to protest and then decide that lying will only make things worse. "Why do you say that?" you ask, frowning. "And how did you know I didn't drown them?"

"I found these outside your door this morning," Russell says, stretching out his hand.

In his palm lie two white rattles.

The End

"I *am* hungry," you say to Karen.

"I thought so," she says. She ladles out a cup of soup and hands it to you. "Go out the back door to eat," she whispers, "so the chef won't see you."

The back door opens on the lodge parking lot. You sit down on the step and start to eat. The soup is delicious. The warm sun is reflecting off the snow. You feel comfortable, almost sleepy. As you watch, a car drives into the lot and two men get out. They seem to be walking strangely. Or is it your eyes? You can't focus!

You blink to clear your vision. By the time the men reach the step, you are almost unconscious. Behind you the kitchen door opens.

"Did it work?" you hear Karen ask.

"Like a charm," replies one of the men. "Let's get you and our guinea pig out of here. We'll get rid of the kid tonight. I'll come back and clean the place out after the guests have had their soup." He laughs. "Sadie's going to be jinxed again!"

"You . . . drugged . . . the . . . soup," you say, struggling for words.

It's the last thing you remember. When you regain consciousness, you're lying on a bed in a small dark room. You stand up and move to a window. It's dark outside. You see neon lights below. You're on the second floor. Slowly the events of the morning come back. You're sure everyone at the lodge was drugged too. And by now, robbed. You're sure of something else as well. Sadie's problems are caused by flesh-and-blood humans, not spirits. But why?

Turn to page 97.

You move to the phone on the nightstand and lift the receiver. There is no dial tone. The cord has been cut. You've got to get out of here! You try the door. It's locked. You go back to the window. There's only a vine clinging to the side of the building. You're not sure it will hold you, but it's worth a try.

You slide the window open and swing yourself out and over, grasping at the vine. Slowly you lower yourself hand over hand as the vine creaks under your weight. Just as your feet hit the ground you hear a shout.

"Hold it!"

What if it's one of the men? you wonder. They said they were going to get rid of you. But it might be someone who could help you. Can you take that chance . . . or should you run?

If you take the chance and answer, turn to page 66.

If you run, turn to page 108.

You explain to the patrolmen why you released the chickens. The two men who kidnapped Heidi are taken into custody.

"How did they capture you in the first place?" you ask her.

"They didn't exactly capture me," Heidi says sheepishly. "I goofed. I hid in the back of the wagon, thinking they were going to the Maple Leaf Inn. Instead, they were going to San Francisco to meet another partner. When they discovered me, they decided to turn around. They figured that if I had an 'unfortunate accident' in the mountains, my death would cause less suspicion than if I was murdered in San Francisco."

"Sadie's going to be surprised to see me back," you say.

"She'll be glad to see you," Heidi says. "And we'll get there just in time for dinner. I think it's barbecued chicken."

"I've had enough chicken for one day," you say. "Let's you and I go to a pizza parlor."

The End

"We've got only one pair of snowshoes," you say to Heidi. "Get on the old toboggan. I'll pull you."

"We'll take turns pulling each other," Heidi says. "Then one person won't get overtired. It'll be faster."

Your ascent is slow. When you finally reach a ridge at the summit, neither Hawkins nor Russell is in sight.

"Let's circle around to the west side," says Heidi. "Give me the snowshoes." She gets off the toboggan and you get on.

You've gone only a little way when Heidi holds up her hand and points. The moon is casting an eerie white light over the scene. Below you on the slope is Hawkins, on skis. He's facing Russell. The hawk perches on Hawkins's outstretched arm, ready to attack.

Turn to page 106.

Before Russell can stop you, you run from the room down the hall. But as you reach the stairs your foot catches in a piece of loose carpet. You lurch forward and end up on the lobby floor.

From behind the desk someone rushes to your side. It's Russell! He covers you with his heavy jacket and calls to someone to call an ambulance.

"How can you be down here and up there too?" you mumble.

"I cannot explain to one who will not hear," he replies.

"I'm listening," you tell him.

"Listening and hearing are quite different," he says.

At the Lake Tahoe hospital they set your broken leg. You stay overnight, and Sadie comes to see you before you leave for home.

"You're the only kid I know," she says, autographing your cast, "who comes to a ski resort and breaks a leg without ever getting on skis."

"Maybe it's the Paiute jinx," you mutter.

"That's Russell's theory," she says softly.

"What would a bellman know about an Indian curse?" you ask.

Turn to page 109.

"Yes, I'll go with you," you tell Russell.

You grab a jacket and follow him out to the van. Snow is falling and the sky is dull gray. You ride without talking, watching the windshield wipers push aside the wet snow. The old van labors as it climbs the steep and narrow mountain road. There are many questions in your mind, some that you're afraid to ask. Finally you break the silence.

"Where are we going?" you ask.

"To Echo Summit," Russell replies, "above the lodge."

"How do you know that's where Hawkins will be?"

"I overheard his final words to Sadie. He said, 'Swiftly the white bird flies at night.'"

"That doesn't tell me anything," you say. "What do you think it means?"

Russell pulls into a rest area and turns off the motor.

"It means," he says solemnly, "that Hawkins is going to trigger an avalanche."

You feel as if someone has squeezed all the air out of you. "And wipe out Echo Lodge," you say softly.

Russell nods. "We'll have to walk from here. The road above will be clogged."

He reaches behind the driver's seat and pulls out some snowshoes. "Put these on," he tells you.

Turn to page 18.

There's no time to be ingenious and fool around with chickens. The truck is moving slowly up the grade, the station wagon a few feet behind you. Only a wire guardrail separates the road and the canyon. Your aim must be perfect.

You squat, preparing yourself for the jump. It's no different than a standing broad jump, you rationalize. You take a deep breath and spring. Your aim is perfect, but something goes wrong.

As you jump, the truck veers to the right to avoid a rock in the road. You miss the car hood and crash into the guardrail, somersaulting over it—down, down to the canyon floor.

The traffic jam that results from your accident is horrendous. Everything on the road stops. When the highway patrolmen arrive to investigate, Heidi is able to escape from the men in the station wagon.

They are eventually found guilty of both kidnapping and malicious mischief. Maple Leaf Inn closes down forever.

Sadie's problems are over.

In a way, so are yours.

The End

Which way did Russell go? The snow at the forest's edge has been trampled, both to the left and the right. Inside its dark confines, the towering redwoods have shielded the ground so the surface is covered, not with snow, but with brown needles and pinecones and rotting branches. It's impossible to tell which way Russell went!

If you go to the left, turn to page 6.

If you go to the right, turn to page 73.

You go back to the sink and angrily start scrubbing potatoes. The chef hones a carving knife. Neither of you speaks.

Suddenly a shriek breaks the silence. Mary comes rushing into the kitchen. She is trembling.

"The guests are all unconscious!" she whispers. "And two masked men with guns just came into the lobby."

Without a word the chef goes to the swinging doors of the kitchen and opens one a crack so he can see into the dining room.

"They're robbing the guests," he whispers. "Watches, rings, wallets—everything!"

"Check on the kitchen help," you hear a man say.

Turn to page 112.

"We'll never be able to stop the hawk," Heidi whispers.

"I'm going to try," you say. You yank the tow rope from her hands and push off before she can stop you. You and the toboggan hurtle down the slope toward Hawkins.

He looks up, startled, but you overshoot your mark, sliding fifty feet past him before you can stop. Fearful, you look back up, expecting to see Russell under attack. Instead, what you see is Russell with his arms raised to the sky.

Suddenly there is a muffled roar. From a ridge above the men a mountain lion springs. It hits Hawkins in the back, knocking him down in the snow. At the same time the lion grabs the hawk in his mouth and starts shaking it. Feathers fly, and the hawk screams as the cat mauls it. Hawkins writhes on the ground as if in pain.

Finally the hawk stops struggling. The cat tosses it aside. Hawkins lies very still and quiet on the white snow.

Turn to page 118.

Without even glancing back, you start to run. All you can think about is getting away and back to Echo Lodge. You're so intent on escaping that you don't hear the motor start, and with its lights off, you don't see the car coming.

It moves faster than you do.

The driver of the hit-and-run vehicle is never found. Sadie is sued by all the guests who were drugged. Shortly after your "accident," Echo Lodge goes into bankruptcy. A year later, the boarded-up lodge is purchased for a small sum by three partners—two men and a woman named Karen.

The woman, a former chemist, supervises all the kitchen help and plans the menus. Soup is one of her specialties.

The End

Sadie sighs. "Russell is a member of the Pit River Indian tribe," she says. "At times I've suspected that he might even be a shaman—a person with supernatural powers."

You take a deep breath. "I think the supernatural is very convenient," you tell her. "I'm going to tell my friends that the Paiute jinx is responsible for my broken leg."

"Why would you do that?" she asks.

"It's better than admitting I'm a klutz," you say, laughing. But your laugh is feeble, and part of you always wonders how Russell could have been in two places at once.

The End

You know you'll never survive the icy waters of Lake Tahoe. Better to wait and see how you can protect yourself inside the launch.

Al pulls at the wheel and heads the craft into a bay. Ahead, lit by the flickering headlights, you think you see a forest.

"What's that?" you ask.

"That's your destination," says Al. "Emerald Island. Beautiful, mysterious, and uninhabited. You'll have it all to yourself. Except for the ghosts."

He inches the boat up to a rickety dock, and the man with the gun gives you a push. "Get goin', kid," he says.

You're not going to argue with a gun, but your mind is working quickly. You close your fingers around the flashlight on the padded seat and push it up under your vest when you stand up. Then you scramble off the boat, up on to the dock.

Go on to the next page.

The boat backs away and heads for shore. Within minutes it's out of sight on the dark lake. The chill wind coming off the water cuts through your jacket, and you wrap your arms around yourself and tuck your hands under your armpits to keep them warm. The spray kicked up by the boat has frozen on your clothes. Your jeans feel like iced cardboard.

The forest would give you some protection from the cold wind, but it's so dark in there. Surely by now Aunt Sadie has someone looking for you. But who'd look on an island out in the lake?

Maybe you could signal with the flashlight from the dock.

*If you choose to go into the forest,
turn to page 63.*

*If you decide to stay on the dock,
turn to page 116.*

112

The chef quickly steps back and lets the door glide shut. He motions to you. When the door opens again, you're ready.

You let fly with a potato. Then another. And another.

The startled gunman drops his weapon. Quickly Mary kicks it under the stove, while the chef grabs the gunman. He wrestles him to the floor and sits on him.

You know the other gunman will come to check on his friend. The chef's busy holding the man on the floor. It's up to you. You grab another potato. When the door opens, you aim for the gun. It hits the floor, but Mary can't get to it. In desperation, she snatches a pepper shaker from the stove. As the gunman lunges she tosses the pepper at him.

Choking and wiping his eyes, he runs for the back door.

Turn to page 46.

You reach the lower slope and look back up at Hawkins. He's skiing swiftly off to the right. Far, far above you looms a gigantic overhang of snow. Even as you watch helplessly, the overhang breaks loose from the mountain and falls slowly, deliberately, toward the slope, where it will pick up tons of snow and continue its descent down the mountain.

The white bird is in flight. The avalanche has started. And you, the cabin—where Heidi may be captive—and Echo Lodge are all in its path.

How long do you have? Thirty seconds? A minute? You shuffle as quickly as you can to a large rock jutting from the side of the mountain. You crouch at its base, hoping for a miracle.

A roaring noise fills your head as the avalanche approaches. Small rocks and chunks of ice fly through the air, bombarding you as you flatten yourself against the boulder. What if it, too, is picked up and tossed down the mountain? You close your eyes as the roar gets louder and you wrap your arms around the rock. It seems as if you are being hit on all sides by flying objects.

Turn to page 117.

"Sure! Hop in back," the driver tells you.

You look into the cab. Besides the driver there are two kids and two dogs sitting on the seat. You climb in between the chicken crates in the bed of the truck. The driver pulls out into traffic.

Heidi and the men have a good head start. But as you reach the outskirts of Placerville your spirits rise. The red station wagon pulls out from a gas station just as you pass and starts following you up the grade.

Heidi is in the front seat. You stare at her, wishing—willing her to look up at you. If ESP ever works, this is the time you need it. You think she sees you, but you aren't sure.

Heidi raises her hand to push her hair back, and you lean forward to catch any signal she might give. Slowly, almost casually, she lowers her hand to her neck and deliberately draws one finger across her throat. She repeats the gesture.

You know what that means. They are going to kill her.

Suddenly the station wagon's turn signal starts flashing. They're going to turn left. You must stop them, but how?

You can jump on the hood, but if your aim isn't perfect, you'll end up in the canyon. You look at the chicken crates. Maybe the chickens can help you.

If you decide to jump on the hood, turn to page 103.

If you decide to use the chickens, turn to page 86.

Better to stay on the dock, you decide, where there's some chance of being seen. You wave the flashlight in the air for a while, and then stomp up and down on the rickety platform, humming one of the songs you learned in marching band.

Once you think you see a light out on the lake, and you frantically wave your flashlight. But the light disappears and, along with it, your hopes. Waves are crashing into the wooden pilings, and the wind howls. You'll never last till morning. You're tired and cold and hungry. You sit down and try to keep yourself awake by counting the waves as they rhythmically slap the deck.

"830 . . . 831 . . . 832 . . ."

Your head nods, and you know you're slipping into a sleep from which you'll never wake. It doesn't matter much now. You curl up with your knees under your chin and wait to die. Your eyes close and you drift into sleep.

You don't know how long you've been sleeping, when you are startled into consciousness by an annoying clattering sound. You open your eyes. A floodlight is washing over the dock and above you a helicopter hovers.

Are you dreaming? Are you dying?

You can't be dreaming. A ladder drops from the helicopter, and a very familiar figure descends quickly.

"Heidi!" you yell, as she drops to the wooden platform.

"We'll get you back to the lodge now, kid," she says, pulling you to your feet.

Turn to page 45.

The roar diminishes and you open your eyes.

The avalanche is still moving down the mountain, but it has veered to the right! The cabin and Echo Lodge will be spared. You have been spared! Trembling, you sit down in the snow.

"We must go now and get Heidi," a voice says.

You look up. Russell is standing over you. Still shaking, you reach out for his extended hand. He pulls you to your feet.

"You changed its path," you whisper, hardly able to breathe. "You changed the path of the avalanche."

Turn to page 77.

You watch in disbelief as Russell motions to the mountain lion. It slinks off into a wooded area. Then you climb back up the slope to join Russell and Heidi.

"Talk about luck!" Heidi says to Russell. "You would have been dead if that lion hadn't shown up. It made short work of the shaman's magic hawk too."

"Is he dead?" you ask Russell in a frightened whisper as you stare at Hawkins's body.

"Yes," Russell replies softly.

"But the cat just knocked him down!" you say. You can feel tears welling up in your eyes. You've never seen someone die before. "I thought shamans were immortal."

"Poor guy probably had a heart attack," Heidi says. "I almost did myself."

Russell gently puts Hawkins's body on the toboggan. "Let's go now," he says.

"Wait!" you say. "Shouldn't we at least bury the hawk?" You turn to the place where the lion dropped the bird's carcass.

It's gone. There's not a feather! Not one drop of blood! The snow is not even disturbed.

"Where's the hawk?" you ask Russell in a choked voice.

"It is our spirits that are immortal," Russell says quietly. "Come now. Let's go back to the lodge."

The End

ABOUT THE AUTHOR

LOUISE MUNRO FOLEY is the author of many books for young readers, including *The Lost Tribe* and *The Mystery of the Highland Crest* in the Choose Your Own Adventure series. She has also written a newspaper column, and her articles have appeared in the *Christian Science Monitor, The Horn Book,* and *Writer's Digest.* Ms. Foley has won several national awards for writing and editing. In addition to writing, she has hosted shows on radio and television in the United States and Canada. A native of Toronto, Ontario, Canada, Ms. Foley now lives in Sacramento, California. She has two sons.

ABOUT THE ILLUSTRATOR

DON HEDIN was the first artist for the Choose Your Own Adventure series, working under the name of Paul Granger, and has illustrated over twenty-five books in the series. For many years, Mr. Hedin was associated with *Reader's Digest* as a staff illustrator and then as art editor. With his wife, who is also an artist, Mr. Hedin now lives in Oak Creek Canyon, Arizona, where he continues to work as a fine arts painter and illustrator.

CHOOSE YOUR OWN ADVENTURE ®

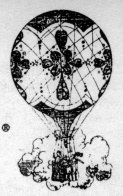

"You'll want all the books in the exciting Choose Your Own Adventure series. Each book takes you through dozens of fantasy adventures—under the sea, in a space colony, into the past—in which *you* are the main character. What happens next in the story depends on the choices *you* make, and *only you* can decide how the story ends!"

☐	23349	SPACE PATROL #22 J. Goodman	$1.95
☐	23366	THE LOST TRIBE #23 L. Foley	$1.95
☐	23733	LOST ON THE AMAZON #24 R. A. Montgomery	$1.95
☐	23661	PRISONER OF THE ANT PEOPLE #25 R. A. Montgomery	$1.95
☐	23635	THE PHANTOM SUBMARINE #26 R. Brightfield	$1.95
☐	23867	THE HORROR OF HIGH RIDGE #27 Julius Goodman	$1.95
☐	23868	MOUNTAIN SURVIVAL #28 Edward Packard	$1.95
☐	23865	TROUBLE ON PLANET EARTH #29	$1.95
☐	23937	THE CURSE OF BATTERSLEA HALL #30	$1.95
☐	24099	VAMPIRE EXPRESS #31	$1.95
☐	24050	TREASURE DIVER #32	$1.95
☐	24249	THE DRAGON'S DEN #33 Richard Brightfield	$1.95
☐	24344	THE MYSTERY OF HIGHLAND CREST #34 Louise Foley	$1.95
☐	24484	JOURNEY TO STONEHENGE #35 Fred Graver	$1.95
☐	24522	THE SECRET TREASURE OF TIBET #36 Richard Brightfield	$1.95
☐	24523	WAR WITH THE EVIL POWER MASTER #37 R. A. Montgomery	$1.95
☐	24678	SUPERCOMPUTER #39 Edward Packard	$1.95
☐	24679	THE THRONE OF ZEUS #40 D. L. Goodman	$1.95
☐	24745	SEARCH FOR MOUNTAIN GORILLAS #41 Jim Wallace	$1.95
☐	24720	THE MYSTERY OF ECHO LODGE #42	$1.95

Prices and availability subject to change without notice.